The Day When Daisy Learned To Dance

HOLLY BEEBEE

Dedication

This book is dedicated to my mother for always encouraging me to write and filling me with wonderful bedtime stories as a child.

WHILE DAISY TOOK A
LITTLE NAP,
SHE SUDDENLY HEARD A
"TAP, TAP, TAP."

TAP!
TAP!
TAP!

WHAT ON EARTH IS
HAPPENING HERE?
THE SOUND WAS GETTING
VERY NEAR.

AND WITH THE SUDDEN
"TAP, TAP" SOUND,
THERE'S MAGIC MUSIC ALL
AROUND.

THE MUSIC HAD A CRAZY BEAT, AND THEN SHE SAW THE DANCING FEET.

CHILDREN DANCING TO
AND FRO,
SOME SOAR HIGH AND
SOME DIP LOW.

THEY WERE IN A
JOYFUL TRANCE
AS THEIR FEET JUST DANCED
AND DANCED.

"DAISY!" SAID THE LITTLE BOY. "DANCE WITH US AND FIND YOUR JOY!"

"BUT I'VE NEVER
DANCED BEFORE.
I'LL BE A FOOL THERE
ON THE FLOOR!"

"IT DOESN'T MATTER, JUST
HAVE FUN,
JOIN IN HERE WITH
EVERYONE! ONCE YOU
HEAR THE CRAZY BEAT, YOU
CANNOT HELP BUT MOVE
YOUR FEET."

DAISY SLOWLY FOUND THE GROOVE. HER HAPPY PAWS WERE ON THE MOVE.

TAP

THE MUSIC TOOK HER FOR A RIDE. SHE COULDN'T HELP BUT BURST WITH PRIDE.

AND WITH THIS PRIDE,
SHE FELT SO FREE.
FREE TO DANCE THERE
JOYFULLY.
SHE DIDN'T HAVE TO
HOLD BACK NOW.
THE CRAZY BEAT JUST
SHOWED HER HOW!

THE CHILDREN CIRCLED
AROUND THAT NIGHT.
A DANCING DOG WAS
QUITE A SIGHT!

THEY'D NEVER SEEN A DOG
DO THIS AND FALL INTO A
DANCING BLISS.

SOON THEY ALL SAT
DOWN TO REST.
THEY'D ABSOLUTELY
DANCED THEIR BEST!

THEY'LL NOT FORGET THE
JOYFUL TRANCE
THE DAY WHEN DAISY LEARNED
TO DANCE!

AUTHOR BIO

Holly loves to write, sing and dance and currently resides in a small town in Pennsylvania. She has been writing poetry for over forty years and often finds herself thinking in rhythm and rhyme.

She has fond memories of her childhood with her parents reading to her before bed and wanted to create fun stories for children that include a message. She hopes you enjoyed reading about Daisy the dog and what she learned along the way!